THIS BOOK BELONGS TO

Boy on a Kite

This edition published in 2005
by Nevis International Books, Atlantic House, Island of Seil, near Oban, Argyll PA34 4RF

Designed by Ruth Bayley.

A catalogue record of this book is available from the British Library.

ISBN 09550778-1-8

Printed in Scotland by www.nevisprint.co.uk

BOY ON A KITE

BY MARK SCOTT

ILLUSTRATED BY RUTH BAYLEY

DEDICATION

The Author dedicates this Book to his Grandson James Angus Steiner, a Child of the New Millennium.

ACKNOWLEDGEMENTS

The Author and Illustrator are appreciative of the advice and assistance of Dr Eleanor Murray Steiner as Literary Consultant. Special thanks also to Andrew McKenna and the production team at Scotland's notable printers, Nevisprint of Fort William.

*I*t's Jamie's birthday and he hopes for a bicycle to ride faster than he can run and glide faster than the wind.

But Mother says she is baking him a birthday cake with seven candles instead.

And Father says he will make him a kite and Jamie can help make it. So they find a large sheet of brown wrapping paper, two bamboo sticks, some glue and Mother's ball of string.

Father put it all on the kitchen table and cut the paper into a diamond shape. Then he tied the two sticks together crosswise and glued them to the paper. Next they made the kite's tail with a strip of sister Meg's pink hair ribbon with bows of paper.

brown paper

bamboo sticks

stick together

ribbon

coloured paper bows – tie on ribbon

Jamie then got his crayons and drew a face on the kite and called him Kit. This made the kite smile saying "I'm Kit the Kite." And "I'm Jamie," the boy replied.

Mother and Meg watched at the garden gate as Father and Jamie carried Kit to the field outside their house. Father held up the kite at arms' length as high as he could while Jamie clutched the long line of twine.

In the gentle breeze Kit smiled as he rose out of Father's fingers and lightly fluttered in the wind. Then he gently floated above Jamie before rapidly gliding skywards like a soaring bird.

Kit flapped his wings and waggled his tail as he mounted upon the wind and climbed higher upwards to the clouds, tugging at Jamie's line. Jamie held on tightly.

Then…twang…zip…the line snapped and the kite was free.

Kit flew across the field and further skywards towards the clouds and the sun. Jamie was left holding the broken string. He felt like crying but held back the tears. Kit flew further away.

Jamie and Father ran across the field after Kit. Sister Meg and Mother joined in the chase with Nell and Jamie calling "Come back, Kit, come back. Don't fly away."

The kite seemed to hear them and somersaulted head
over tail in a gust of wind. Kit slowly floated earthwards
in slow circles and landed softly on the meadow grass.
The cows tossed their heads, shook their tails and ran
away from the kite in fright.

Jamie ran as fast as a rabbit to the kite. Breathlessly he picked
up Kit and held the kite tightly so he would not fly away
again. "I don't like being tied to string" Kit told Jamie.
"I like flying free as an eagle."

Then Mother called to them all that
it was time to come home for tea
and Jamie's birthday cake.

Jamie proudly carried Kit back to the house and told Grandmother how Kit flew like a bird. Grandma said she would find some stronger string to keep Kit on the line and not fly away again.

As it was Jamie's birthday, Mother said Jamie could take Kit up to his bedroom at bedtime.

So after all the excitement of chasing Kit across the field, as well as the birthday fun, the party games and blowing out the seven candles, Jamie wearily climbed up the creaky wooden stairs to bed with Kit. Jamie placed the kite by the bedside. "Please don't tie me to the string" said Kit, "I like to be free like a bird."

"Alright" said Jamie. "But don't fly out of the window."

While Jamie was closing his eyes, Kit also looked sleepy. They both yawned and yawned as they slumbered deep and deeper away into Dreamland.

In Slumberland, Jamie and Kit dreamed they would soar like an eagle, lighter than air, high in the sky.

FLYING NORTH TO SCOTLAND

In Slumberland Jamie and Kit's Dreamtime Adventure is to soar like an eagle, lighter than air, high in the sky.

After a busy day at school and after he had finished his homework, Jamie went to bed early. He placed Kit by the window. Jamie was deeply asleep in Dreamland when he heard a fluttering of wings on the glass window pane.

"What are you doing?" yawned Jamie.

Kit replied "Just as children get itchy feet when they want to run and play – so I get itchy wings when I want to fly and play in the sky."

"But I don't get itchy feet" muttered Jamie, "because I wash my feet in the shower every day."

Kit sighed "Well you know what I mean." But Jamie shook his head. "No, I don't know what you mean. You should say what you mean and mean what you say."

Kit nodded "You are quite right, Jamie. what I mean is – let's have another adventure. I can fly high in the sky and give you an eagle's eye look at the world." Jamie quickly put on his woolly scarf and warm gloves. "We shall fly to the North, to the home of the North Wind and the land of eagles and snowy mountains" said Kit.

As Jamie dressed he told the Kite what he had learned at school about eagles. These Kings of the snowy mountain peaks, fly as free as the Lord of the Winds.

"We too shall sail on the wind like an eagle" said Kit who opened the window and waited for Jamie in the garden.

"Now hold on tightly" said Kit. Jamie clutched the Kite who wrapped his tail firmly around Jamie. Kit faced into the breeze and rose up and up skywards above the rooftop, over the garden tree and beyond the Church spire. The steeple weathercock spun round in surprise as the Boy on the Kite glided upwards.

Jamie clutched on tighter and told Kit "Don't let me fall." Kit wrapped his ribbon tail around Jamie even tighter and replied "Don't be frightened. The fear of doing something is sometimes worse than doing it. It's like learning to ride a bicycle or swimming. It's easier when you are careful and not alone." Jamie held on even tighter as Kit soared north to Scotland and the Highlands.

"We shall soon see the highest mountain in Britain called Ben Nevis" said Kit.

Jamie remembered his Scottish Grandma telling him that "A Ben is what the Highlanders call a Mountain. Lakes are called lochs and cottages are crofts and boys are laddies and girls are lassies."

Jamie couldn't wait to see the Highlands with the red deer with their big antlers, the shaggy Highland cattle, the little Shetland ponies and, of course, the fierce Golden Eagles.

Soon the Boy on the Kite could see far below a noisy train taking
tourists from London to Inverness for Highland holidays.

Kit could also see Scottish shepherds with their flocks of woolly sheep
and he could hear the skirl of the bagpipes on the castle walls.

They glided over the snow capped Bens with their green mountainside
fir forests which shelter the homes of red foxes and grey squirrels.

They then glided towards an immense gleaming lake called Loch
Ness which was like a giant's mirror that reflects the Bens. Above
the loch a great rainbow curved across the sky like a dazzling
arched bridge painted in a myriad of colours.

Jamie called out to Kit "Fly to the top of the rainbow
and let me slide down it."
"Alright" replied Kit. "But don't fall off."
"Is it true there's a pot of gold at the end of the rainbow?"
asked Jamie.
Kit laughed and waggled his tail and said "We'll see what's at
the rainbow's end."

Jamie climbed onto the rainbow which was so bright he could feel
the colours, the warm red, cool blue, tingly yellow, glossy green.
Then Jamie started to slide down and down, faster and faster until
he tumbled to a halt at the bottom.

There was no pot of gold there, but there was a big grey heron
standing like a statue watching a plump frog in the mud.

Jamie didn't want the heron to catch the frog
so he jumped on Kit and the Boy on the Kite
skimmed over the loch, where Jamie saw
an otter scrambling over the pebbles while
a family of squawking ducks splashed
in the water.

An Angler was fishing for a big brown trout in a pool by the tree-lined waterside. When the fisherman saw the Boy on the Kite he was so startled that he dropped his fishing rod in the water and the big trout swam away to the deep dark waters of the loch. Kit said "The Highlanders say a monster called Nessie lives in the loch." Jamie shivered and said "Well let's hurry away."

Kit flew up and up towards a fluffy white candy floss cloud which
was like a huge bouncy cotton wool balloon as white as snow.
The cloud moved quickly away and the skies darkened like a
grey blanket.

Suddenly a great Golden Eagle swooped down like an arrow from the mountain peak and hovered like a black shadow over the kite and Jamie. The Great Bird, the Lord of the Mountains, was so close that Jamie could see his cruel talons, and fierce beak. His bright eye, which could see a mouse miles away, stared at the kite. Jamie could feel Kit was trembling with fright – so Jamie held on even more tightly to the Kite and he also began to tremble. The Eagle came closer and opened his sharp beak and said "Don't be frightened – I won't hurt you." Then he shook his great wings. "I've come to tell you to hurry home because a storm is coming and soon the land will be covered with Scotch mist and rain. So go home while you can. Come back another day when the storm has gone and the sun is shining on the snowy Highlands."

Jamie and the kite thanked the Eagle and Kit hurriedly turned southwards and raced home before they got lost in the Scotch mist and darkness.

Below them the cities with their street lamps looked like toy towns. And on they flew towards the dawn sunrise. In the gardens and fields the birds started singing their dawn chorus to awaken the sun.

As the sun climbed up above the horizon, the lights came on in the tiny houses below as people awakened for breakfast and hurried to get ready for school and work.

Kit arrived with Jamie at home just in time to wake up for breakfast.

Jamie told the family about his dreamland flight to the North and meeting the Golden Eagle Bird.

Grandma said Jamie had eaten too much Birthday cake yesterday which made him dream so much last night.

Kit just smiled in the corner of the kitchen and was planning the next dreamland flight.

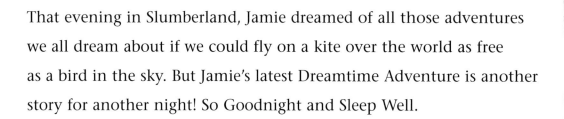

That evening in Slumberland, Jamie dreamed of all those adventures we all dream about if we could fly on a kite over the world as free as a bird in the sky. But Jamie's latest Dreamtime Adventure is another story for another night! So Goodnight and Sleep Well.

OVER THE SEAS TO THE WESTERN ISLES

In their last Slumberland Adventure, Jamie and Kit flew North to Scotland to meet the Golden Eagle, the King of the Mountains. The Eagle had warned them to fly home quickly before the rainstorm came and to return another day when the sun is shining. So Jamie hurried home. Now he dreams of flying back to the Highlands on the way to the Western Isles on the wings of Kit the Kite.

They were not asleep long in Dreamland before Jamie and Kit
agreed to return to the snow covered Highlands.

Jamie put on his warm, fleecy hat, his woolly scarf and Grandma's
knitted mittens.

He held on tightly as the kite glided high above the clouds over
Ben Nevis mountain.

The Golden Eagle was hovering high in the blue sky waiting for
the Boy on the Kite. His Eagle eye spotted them long before
Jamie saw him. Then the Eagle swooped down from the heights
and greeted Jamie. "Ceud Mile Failte" said the Eagle in the
Scottish language of Gaelic which means "A Hundred
Thousand Welcomes."

Kit and Jamie were pleased the Eagle was
still friendly because Eagles like to be
Kings of the Mountains and rule
the skies alone.

On the mountain sides skiers were racing down the ski-
slopes and the mountaineers were climbing to the icy
mountain top. Down in the village children were
sledging or throwing snowballs at a snowman.
Then snowflakes the size of pennies floated gently
down like confetti from the cold sky. Kit shivered
and shook ice off his tail and Jamie pulled
his fleecy hat over his ears and tightened
his scarf.

"Let's fly over to the
mountainside ski-lodge
and get warm" said Jamie.

The lodge was a large wooden restaurant called "The Snowgoose".
Inside, skiers, climbers and sledgers were warming themselves by the
log fire with mugs of hot chocolate and ovenfresh buttered
scones or warm bread and Scotch broth.

Everyone was cheerfully exchanging stories of their mountain adventures. Outside a roar like thunder made everyone look out of the windows to watch a large yellow helicopter ambulance on its way to rescue a skier with a broken leg and take him to the local Fort William Hospital.

As it got colder on the mountain, a friendly Highlander advised Kit and Jamie to fly over to the warm west coast where the warm gulf stream of the seas kept the land free from frost and snow. So Jamie and Kit waved "Goodbye" to the mountain folk in the ski-lodge and flew towards the seaport of Oban and the Western Isles.

On the way, Kit flew low
over a little Highland croft.
Outside an old, white haired lady
was looking up at a tall fir tree.
She was pointing to her woollen
shawl that had blown off her washing
line and was hanging on a high branch.
Kit floated down to the tree and Jamie
rescued the shawl and dropped it down
to the crofter lady's outstretched hands.
She was so pleased she clapped her hands
with glee and invited Jamie and Kit
into her cosy home.

She told them she was Mrs MacTavish and her cottage was called "An Tigh" which means in English "The House". She explained it was her best Sunday Shawl that she had knitted during the long winter nights.

The Highland Lady happily wrapped her shawl around her and rewarded Jamie with a tasty lunch of grilled herring, boiled buttered potatoes and freshly baked oatcakes while Kit stayed close to the logfire to melt the snow off his wings and tail.

As they all said their farewells, Mrs MacTavish said in her soft Highland voice "Haste Ye Back – come and see me again."

Jamie promised to return and bring her a fresh
lobster from Oban fish market on their way home.

As Kit flew over Oban, fishing boats in
the harbour were unloading nets of silvery
fish, pink crabs and blue lobsters.

Seagulls were flocking over the trawlers to snatch a
fish and the townswomen were at the fishmarket buying
fish for their families' suppers.

Kit hovered over the town and wheeled about as the fisherfolk
watched with curiosity the Boy on the Kite.

Jamie could smell the appetising seafood and fried fish cooking in
the seafront Fish Restaurant called Ee-usk which is Gaelic for "fish".

Jamie felt hungry and wanted to eat and then explore Oban's
Lifeboat Station and sailing ships. Jamie could understand why the
old town is called "The Gateway to the Isles" as the Ferry ships
with tourists and Islanders cruised in and out of the Port to the
islands of Mull, Islay, Colonsay and Skye.

Kit followed a Ferry called "Lord of the Isles" out to sea. On the way
Jamie spotted a fishing boat and as they glided over the boat, the
fisherman waved to them and called on The Boy on the Kite to come
down and join him.

The old seaman introduced himself as Skipper McColl and welcomed
them into his small cabin. The Skipper lit his pipe and puffed out smelly
blue smoke while he brewed a pot of tea. He said he had never seen a
Boy on a Kite before and he smiled when he remarked that he would
rather sail on the stormy seas than glide on the winds, because he could
swim but he couldn't fly like a bird or a kite and he didn't like heights.

While he drank his mug of tea and stroked his beard Skipper McColl said he must catch fish to sell in the market. He asked Jamie if he would like to help him catch the mackerel. He gave Jamie a rod and line with six hooks on it. Skipper dropped his line in the cold grey sea and he told Jamie to do likewise.

Suddenly the old fisherman pulled up his fishing rod and reeled in the line on which two ten inch long silvery blue mackerel were wriggling on the hooks. Jamie jumped with excitement as the fish were hauled into the boat where Skipper packed them in a box of crushed ice.

Skipper told Jamie to stop rocking the boat and to drop his line into the sea and to jiggle the line up and down to attract the fish. Jamie jiggled the rod up and down until he felt a sharp jerk on the line which nearly pulled him overboard.

"Help me, help me" shouted Jamie. "I've caught a monster fish."

But Skipper just stroked his beard and told Jamie to reel in the line which was being tugged down and bending the fishing rod till it nearly snapped. "It's a real monster" yelled Jamie while Skipper was busy dropping his own line back into the sea.

"Keep reeling in the fish Jamie" replied the Skipper.
Jamie was getting breathless as he hauled in the heavy
tugging line as the fishing rod bent even more. With one
great heave he hauled the line out of the water and there –
there were five big silvery mackerel on the hooks.
"Well done Jamie" shouted Skipper. "Now pull the fish
into the boat quickly before they wriggle off the hooks."

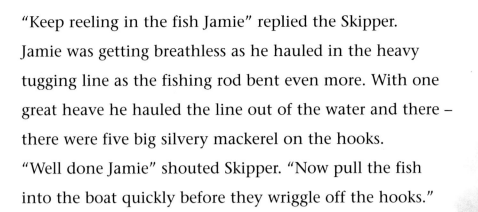

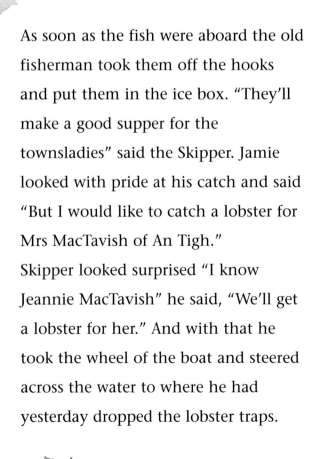

As soon as the fish were aboard the old
fisherman took them off the hooks
and put them in the ice box. "They'll
make a good supper for the
townsladies" said the Skipper. Jamie
looked with pride at his catch and said
"But I would like to catch a lobster for
Mrs MacTavish of An Tigh."
Skipper looked surprised "I know
Jeannie MacTavish" he said, "We'll get
a lobster for her." And with that he
took the wheel of the boat and steered
across the water to where he had
yesterday dropped the lobster traps.

He stopped the boat and hauled aboard the orange ball which was a buoy marking where the lobster creel had been dropped. When the Skipper opened the trap, a big blue lobster with a large pincer crawled out and tried to nip Kit's tail. Kit jumped up and said "Let's fly off. I don't want to be nipped." Skipper grabbed the lobster and put it in a shoulder bag and gave it to Jamie to take back to Mrs MacTavish.

As Kit prepared to fly off the boat, Jamie looked over the
side at the blue jelly fish floating in the green water. Suddenly
there was a great splash as a large grey dolphin leapt out of the
sea and plunged up and down around the boat. Skipper threw a
mackerel to the dolphin who leapt out and gulped down the fish.
"I'm glad we didn't catch that beautiful dolphin" said Jamie.
"Aye" said Skipper, "We protect our dolphins. We never
catch them," and he threw another fish to the plunging
dolphin who swam away towards the Island of Mull.
As Kit and Jamie followed the dolphin they saw seals
basking on rocks eating salmon which they had caught
in the deep waters.

As they reached Mull, Kit flew low over the Ferry, "Lord of the Isles",
which was unloading a stream of cars with tourists. The holiday makers
were amazed to see a Boy on a Kite and they waved to Jamie.
"Ceud Mile Failte" Jamie greeted them to practise his newly learned
Gaelic. The Ferryman explained to the tourists "That means a "Hundred
Thousand Welcomes." One tourist wanted to know why Jamie was not
wearing a kilt and the Ferryman explained that the boy was also a
visitor to Scotland. Jamie was so busy waving to everyone that he nearly
dropped the shoulder bag with the lobster for Mrs MacTavish.

Kit scolded Jamie and told him to hold on tightly as he was going to fly up to Ben More mountain. As they soared up towards the peak, Jamie saw an Eagle hovering above the purple heather covered mountainside.

As soon as the red deer, the mountain hares and the pheasants saw the Eagle's dark shadow above them, all the creatures scampered away to hide among the rocks and heather. Then the King of the Mountains suddenly dived down like an arrow with his talons outstretched and swept up a rabbit crouching in the heather. The Eagle soared up to the rocky crags clutching the rabbit in his sharp claws to the Eagle's nest to feed the Mother Eagle and the hungry chick eaglet.

Kit did not want the Eagle to dive on him and Jamie so the kite quickly flew away and glided down to the village far from the Eagle.

There Jamie talked to the village children and showed the laddies and lassies how to make their own kites instead of buying kites in a shop.

Soon it was time to fly home and deliver the lobster to Mrs MacTavish before it became dark.

When they spotted the tall fir
tree at "An Tigh" Jamie landed
on the roof and shouted down
the chimney, "Mrs MacTavish,
we're back." Jamie then dropped
the lobster down the chimney into
the lady's cooking pot.

Mrs Mac thanked Jamie and Kit and
invited them to stay for tea of freshly
baked oatcakes and buttered scones.
But Kit explained they must travel on
homewards before darkness. The
Highland Lady told them "Haste Ye
Back again. I'll knit a nice woollen
scarf to keep you warm up there
in the clouds."

But Jamie said he would rather
she sent her nice woolly scarf
to Skipper McColl to thank
him for his lobster.

As they flew south homewards Jamie shivered and said he wished they had stopped to get warm.

But Kit was so tired after flying so far around the Highlands and Islands that he just wanted to hurry home and to sleep.

That night in bed Jamie yawned and muttered "We've been North with the Eagles and fishing around the Western Isles, so let's go somewhere warm on our next flight."

Kit agreed and, yawning, he said "It's cold on the snowy North mountains and it's windy in the West, so let's fly South and follow the swallows to the sunshine, to the deserts and camels, to see palm trees and warm tropical beaches."

"Yes, yes" mumbled Jamie "We'll go somewhere sunny and exciting," as he snuggled down under his duvet and nodded off to Slumberland for the next Dreamtime Adventure which is tomorrow's story. So Good Night.

FLYING TO THE SUNNY SOUTH WITH SWALLOWS

After their last Dreamtime Adventure flying to the West over the Eagle's snowy mountains, Jamie and Kit agreed to fly South with the Swallows to the sunny lands, to the tropics and a Desert Island in their next Slumberland Adventure.

*I*n Slumberland, Jamie was roused by the chattering of swallows outside his bedroom window. He pulled the Kite's tail. "Wake up Kit" said Jamie, "The swallows are awake and flying back to the Sunny South." Kit blinked, stretched his wings and woke up.

Jamie put on his sunhat and sandals and they hurried outside to the garden to join the bustling swallows. Soon they were winging over London, over the white cliffs of Dover and across the English Channel to France.

The Ships and Ferries looked like toy boats and
Jamie waved to the seagulls gliding over the waves.
"Hold on tight" said Kit. "I will" replied Jamie.
"The green sea looks very cold."

When they reached France, Jamie could see the apple orchards and vineyards with grapes below them on their way to Paris.

The swallows rested on the high Eiffel Tower and beckoned to Kit to rest before they flew across the Mediterranean Sea to Africa.

Down on the Mediterranean beaches, lots of tourists were sunbathing or paddling in the warm blue sea water. As they flew South it became warmer and warmer in the bright sunshine and Jamie was glad to be wearing his sun hat.

The swallows swooped about the sky and zigzagged in flight to catch flies, but Kit flew straight on to Africa and glided down to the palm trees. Jamie happily picked some sticky, sweet dates and gathered some juicy oranges in the orange groves for their thirsty journey over the hot, dry desert.

When Jamie saw the Bedouin desert people with white robes riding camels he wondered how the Arab people could live in such a hot dusty desert. But soon he saw a green oasis with bubbling spring water and more date palm trees where the swallows rested again.

In the shade of the palm trees, the Bedouin Arabs had pitched their tents where the children waved to the Bird Boy on the Kite to come down and join them. The Bedouin children welcomed the skytravellers with glasses of warm, honey sweetened tea and asked Jamie how to make a Kite.

Then they showed Jamie how to climb on to a camel to ride around the oasis while Kit asked an old Bedouin the way to the Pyramids of Egypt. The Bedouin told Kit just to follow the swallows who knew their way even in the dark, when they followed the stars like signposts in the night skies.

Kit told Jamie he wanted to see the Pyramids so they quickly followed the swallows along the River Nile of ancient Egypt.

The Pyramids are huge man-made mountains of stone made thousands of years ago by thousands of slaves for the Pharaoh Kings of Egypt.

Jamie and Kit sat down on a Pyramid and watched the tourists riding camels around the Pyramids or buying souvenirs to take home. It was so hot that all Jamie wanted was a water melon and an ice cream while Kit rested and talked to the swallows about the way across the Equator to the jungles of Africa.

On the way to the jungles, Kit and Jamie flew low over the roaring waterfalls on a very wide river where fierce looking crocodiles were lying like logs in the muddy water. Nearby, elephants and a big hippopotamus were standing in the water to keep cool.

Jamie felt hot in the bright sun but he did not want to paddle in the crocodiles' river, so Kit flew on across the dry bushland where they saw lions and giraffes in the grasslands. When the King of the lions saw Jamie and the kite, the lion roared so loud that the giraffes stopped eating the leaves of the tall trees and they ran away.

In the jungle, monkeys were swinging between the trees and chattering with excitement when a long snake slithered up the branches. The birds looked like brightly coloured parrots and they squawked when they saw Kit hovering over the tree tops. When Jamie saw a leopard sleeping on a branch he decided the jungle was not a place to stop among fierce animals. Kit agreed. Even the swallows did not linger but flew on to a nearby African village.

The village children waved and clapped their hands as they marvelled at Kit and the Bird Boy and shouted to them to fly down and join them. They exchanged stories about why Jamie was white because he lived in a cold country and they were tanned brown by the bright African sun. Jamie gave them one of his oranges and some dates and they gave Jamie some coconuts, peanuts and mangoes before Kit and Jamie said their farewells and flew up to the sky again to rejoin the swallows.

Jamie asked the swallows to show him the way to a Tropical Island where he could swim and Kit could lie down on the warm sand and rest his weary wings.

When they reached the sea they saw a sandy little island in the blue waters. It was quite lonely with only a few coconut trees and no one lived on the deserted desert island. "That's why they are called Desert Islands" Jamie told Kit who was glad they still had some peanuts, dates and oranges in Jamie's knapsack.

As soon as they floated down on the island Kit rested on the beach in the shade of a palm tree while Jamie paddled and splashed in the warm sea water. "Come and join me" Jamie shouted to the swallows flying above him but they shook their heads and said they couldn't swim. So Jamie watched the beautiful blue, yellow and purple fish swimming around his feet in the clear water of the coral reef. Further from the beach he could see flying fish skimming over the waves.

While Kit was fast asleep under a shady palm tree, Jamie explored the Island. He had read at school that pirates buried treasure on desert islands so Jamie hurried and scurried about looking for the Pirates' Treasure chest.

But he found nothing, The Desert Island was deserted except for an old parrot who squawked "The Pirates don't come here any more. They have grown old and they stay at home telling stories of the sea."

As Jamie walked along the beach back to Kit he saw an old green bottle on the white sand. Jamie pulled out the cork and lifted out a piece of paper. On it was a message which said "Whoever finds me will have Good Luck if they don't break the bottle, but put it safely in a Litter Bin."

"But there isn't a Litter Bin here" Jamie told Kit. "Never mind" said Kit. "We'll take it home because tourists should always take their litter home and only leave their footprints on the sand."

whoever finds me shall have good luck if they don't break the bottle but put it safely in a litter bin!

Just then a dark cloud came towards the Island and a loud bang of thunder in the sky frightened the old parrot and the swallows.

As the skies darkened Kit said "We had better hurry home. A tropical storm is coming and soon there will be a heavy rainfall." The swallows agreed and they all chattered "That's right – hurry home before the monsoon rains come."

So Kit and Jamie returned North away from the storm clouds and glided as fast as the wind back home before breakfast.

When they arrived back at their cosy home Jamie said "A Desert Island is nice for a holiday but I wouldn't like to live there. There is no nice clean, fresh water to drink like we have. We can turn on the tap for a glass of water." Kit agreed saying "And we don't get wet from a rainstorm in our warm house." Jamie said "I won't forget to put the bottle in the litter bin in the morning."

So they both tumbled back into their bed again and to sleep until their next Slumberland adventure when they would fly to the East and the Land of the Dragons.

EAST TO THE LAND OF THE DRAGONS

So far in Slumberland, Jamie and Kit have flown North with
the eagles to the cold Highlands, then West to the windswept
Western Isles with the seals and dolphins before gliding
South with the swallows to the sunny tropics. Now Jamie,
the Boy on Kit the Kite, travels East around the compass
to China, the land of the Dragons and Kites.

One evening instead of supper at home, Jamie's father took the family for a treat to their local Chinese restaurant, the Golden Dragon.

Later that night, asleep in their cosy home, Jamie dreamed of China, the Land of the Dragons and Kit dreamed of the Land of the Kites.

So the Boy on the Kite journeyed eastwards in Slumberland to the exciting and mysterious land of China.

They glided over the silver seas, dusty deserts and the snowy Himalayan mountains and flew along the Great Wall of China for 3,000 miles to reach the vast capital city Beijing, which was once called Peking.

Jamie marvelled at the strange shaped Palaces and Temples in the Forbidden City where once no strangers were allowed to visit. It was here that China's Boy Emperor once ruled his great Empire behind the Great Wall of China, which is the longest wall in the world and is the Seventh Wonder of the World. All the strange buildings were protected by fierce looking stone dragons guarding the doors and gates.

Kit circled over the ancient red and gold painted Emperor's Palace with its gardens of white and pink Cherry Blossom trees and unusual plants like tiger lilies, lotus blossom and chestnut, walnut, almond and pear trees.

Jamie said he wanted to talk to the people but Kit said he was
hungry. So they agreed they should have a real Chinese meal in
a real Chinese restaurant.

When Kit glided down to the courtyard of the Emperor's Palace
they were greeted by a Tourist Guide, Mr Wang who said "Ni
hao" – "Hallo" and "Huan Ying" – "You are welcome."

Mr Wang proudly showed them his great city and guided them
through the swarming crowds of cyclists and pedestrians
waving red flags and banging drums and gongs. When Jamie
said he never had seen so many people, Mr Wang explained
that one in every five people in the world is Chinese.

The delicious smell of cooking from the street restaurants made Jamie and Kit even more hungry.

They were delighted when Mr Wang invited them into a real Chinese Chinese restaurant for a real Chinese Chinese meal. The menu had 64 different dishes and although Jamie could count the numbers, he could not read the Chinese words which were written as pictures and not letters of the English alphabet. Mr Wang explained what the picture words meant like boiled and fried rice, tasty noodles, bamboo shoots, water chestnuts, birds' nest and shark's fin soup, savoury snacks, moon cakes and rice paper sweets.

Kit was amazed at the big round table instead of a square table at home. The round table was loaded with delicious dishes of food and pots of Jasmine tea, orange blossom and green tea. The circular turntable could revolve round like a roundabout so everyone could choose what they wanted to eat.

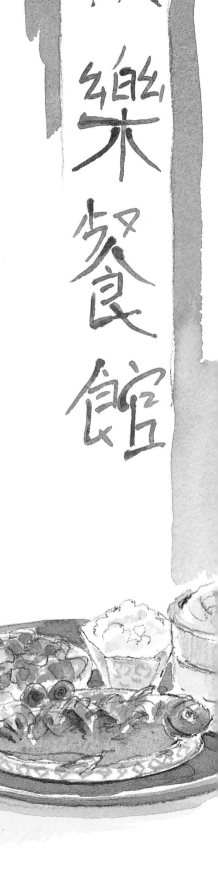

58

But with all this feast of tasty
dishes there was a problem, a real
problem – there were no knives and
forks – only bamboo cane sticks like
long pencils.

Mr Wang explained they were
Chopsticks and Chinese people hold
them in their fingers like tweezers or pincers
to take up small pieces of food to eat – even
small grains of rice or beans and butterfly
prawns. Jamie tried to use the chopsticks but as he
was very hungry he had to ask the waiter for a knife and fork
instead, so he could eat his food.

Kit was enjoying turning the turntable and asking Mr Wang about
dragons and kites.

Mr Wang told them that dragons are for Good Luck and are placed at
the doors of houses to keep away Bad Luck and to guard their homes.

"We also have dragon parades in our streets when our people dress up
like dragons to drive away bad luck from
the streets" said Mr Wang who
added "We even have dragon
Kites to fly high in the sky."

Kit was fascinated when Mr Wang told
them about the different Chinese Dragon
Kites, Box Kites and Bird Kites that are made
of silk, plastic and cloth as well as paper. Mr Wang
smiled with pride when he explained how the Chinese people
invented paper thousands of years ago.

Kit said he wanted to fly off with the Chinese Kites but he would
soon have to go home.

So Mr Wang said "Farewell" "Goodbye" – "Zai jian" to Jamie and
Kit. He wished the Bird Boy a safe journey back home to the
West, to the land of the setting sun, to their land of knives and
forks and their land with no rice fields.

As Kit and Jamie flew along the great Yellow Yangtze River they
saw rice fields where children and adults were standing in the
water covered paddy fields planting rice.

The huge rice fields stretched as far as they could see into the distance.
"No wonder China is called the Rice Bowl of the World" said Kit, "And
why the Chinese eat rice every day of the year" said Jamie, who liked
his Grandmother's weekly rice pudding at home.

Kit was so excited and energetic after their Chinese feast that he
stretched his wings and soared higher and higher up in the blue sky
and through the grey clouds.

Jamie shivered with the cold damp as they passed through the mist and fog of the gloomy clouds.

"We can't see where we are going in all this grey mist" Jamie shouted to Kit. "It's worse than smoke or steam up here."

Just as Jamie said this, there was a sudden frightening roar and rumble, bang and clang as a terrible thunderstorm crashed and smashed all around them. Then a bright red lightning flash streaked fire across the sky which was becoming darker and darker.

Kit cried out in pain as his wing was ripped and torn. "Hold on tight, Jamie" he shouted. "I'm hurt, the lightning has cut my wing."

Jamie clutched Kit's bamboo arms and shivered with fright as well as the high-sky cold. He was frightened that they would fall down and down the sky into the icy cold river and rice fields. "I'm scared" said Jamie. "So am I", said Kit. "But we mustn't get upset or panic."

So Jamie and Kit stayed steady and slowly and carefully glided down away from the grey clouds and the angry thunderstorm to the calm land and safety of a village.

"I'll look after you Kit" said Jamie when he saw the long tear in the Kite's wing. "I'll find a Kite Doctor to mend you."

Down in the village adults as well as children were flying
Kites of every size, shape and colour.

"It's nice to be among my sky family" said Kit as a flock
of Kites greeted them. "And it's nice to be among such
friendly people" said Jamie.

The people in the village playground were enjoying their
usual weekend Kite-flying Display for the Highest Kite.
Jamie waved his woolly scarf and shouted "Ni hao" –
"Hallo" to greet them.

On landing, the villagers welcomed them and stood back to allow the Village Kite Doctor to heal Kit by mending his torn wing with a silk bandage.

The Kite Doctor was the Village Elder with a long white beard and a long blue coat. The wise Old Man was called Li Po.

While the Wise Elder was mending Kit, he said Jamie's father had made the Kite very well – simple, light but strong, very fast and very clever. He told Kit "It's because you are so well made that you were not more badly torn by the thunder and lightning."

Elder Li Po explained the Ancient Chinese Art of Kite Making and Flying. "It's serious work to make a serious Kite that is Master of the Wind and Emperor of the Sky."

Kit stretched his wing and thanked the Kite Doctor for healing him.

Jamie asked the Wise Old Man the way home before the next thunderstorm and before it became dark and night time.

The Elder replied "If you don't know where you are going you won't get there, and if you don't know what you want you won't get it."

Jamie knew they must fly home before the sun dropped down on the horizon in the West and it became dark.

Old Li Po signalled to the village Kites to fly high and guide Kit the safest and quickest way home by following the sun sinking in Jamie's western home.

nd that's how Jamie and Kit arrived back home in time for a snooze and to wake up in time for breakfast and school. Jamie could hardly wait for another adventure with Kit – but that's another story...and another book about a Boy on a Kite.

OWN KITE HERE!

AUTHOR BIOGRAPHY

Mark Scott is the nom de plume of an international journalist, broadcaster and lawyer. He has served on various Tribunals and Councils concerned with justice and social equality. Married with one son, he lives on a Scottish island when not travelling overseas as lawyer and writer. As a yachtsman, his lifelong love and respect for the Sea and islands increases with time, age and each voyage, believing "Nach Uramach an Cuan" "How worthy of honour is the sea".

ILLUSTRATOR BIOGRAPHY

Ruth Bayley is an internationally respected illustrator who has worked as an advertising art director for national press and television. After a professional career in London and Manchester, Ruth Bayley now lives on the Scottish coast, illustrating books and designing graphics.

Together the Scott-Bayley literary collaboration has produced the internationally acclaimed childrens classics "Nell of the Seas" with its sequel "Nell of the Islands" and the commended Swiss "Alpine Legends".